To my extraordinary children,
Jemima & Jordan.

And with thanks to the many hats
who made light work.

First U.S. edition 2014

Library of Congress Catalog Card Number 2013955941
ISBN 978-0-7636-7324-6

TLF 19 18 17 16 15
10 9 8 7 6 5 4 3 2

Printed in Dongguan, Guangdong, China

This book was typeset in My Own Topher.
The illustrations were done in pencil and digital watercolor.

Candlewick Press
99 Dover Street
Somerville, Massachusetts 02144

visit us at www.candlewick.com

There once was a man

named Norman Qwerty...

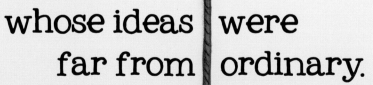

whose ideas were
far from ordinary.

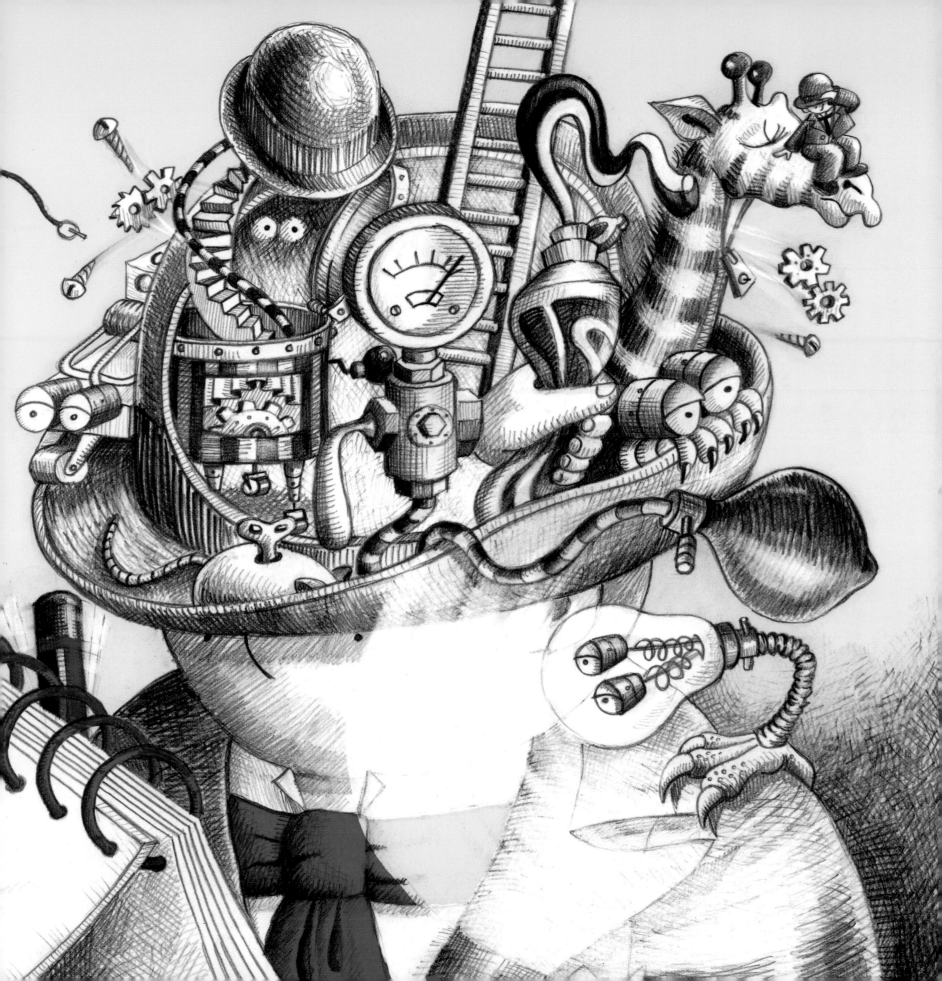

the way that Mr. Qwerty thought....

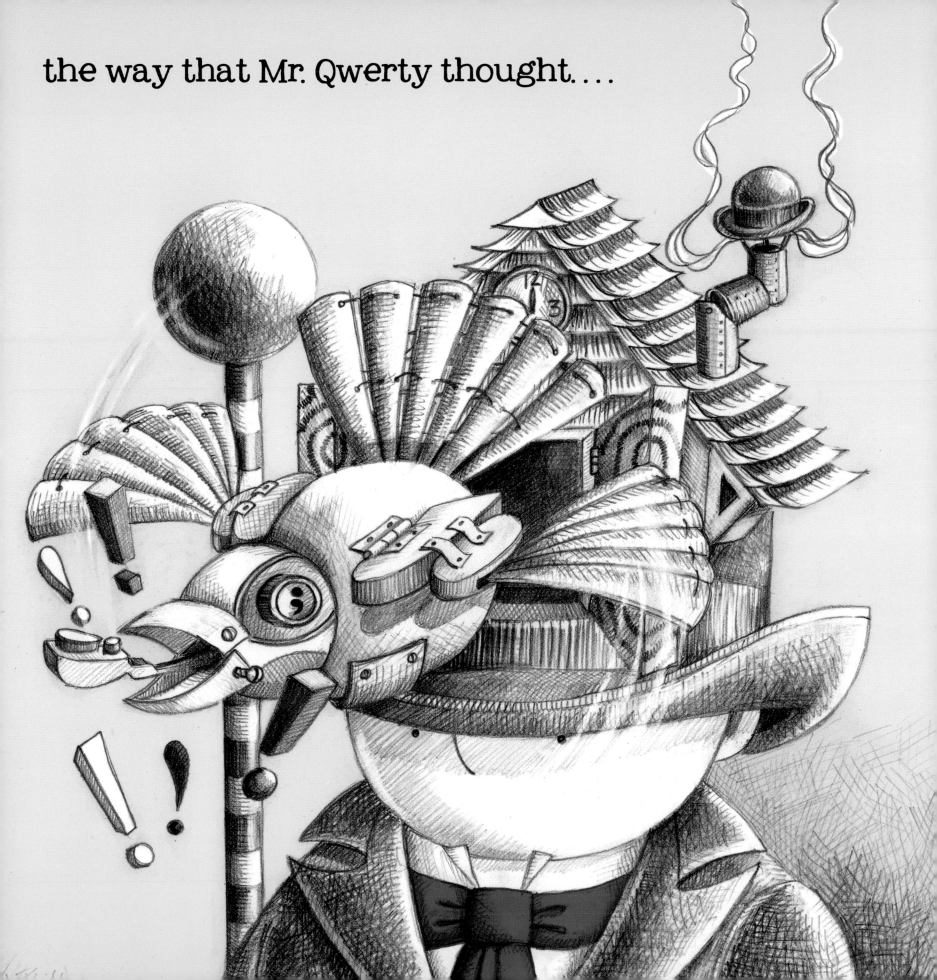

Or so <u>he</u> thought.

Mr. Qwerty was afraid
that people would think
his ideas were strange,

and he felt completely
alone.

most of the time.

as ideas often do,

they GREW,

and GREW,

until they were
SO BIG . . .

that something
had to be done
about them.

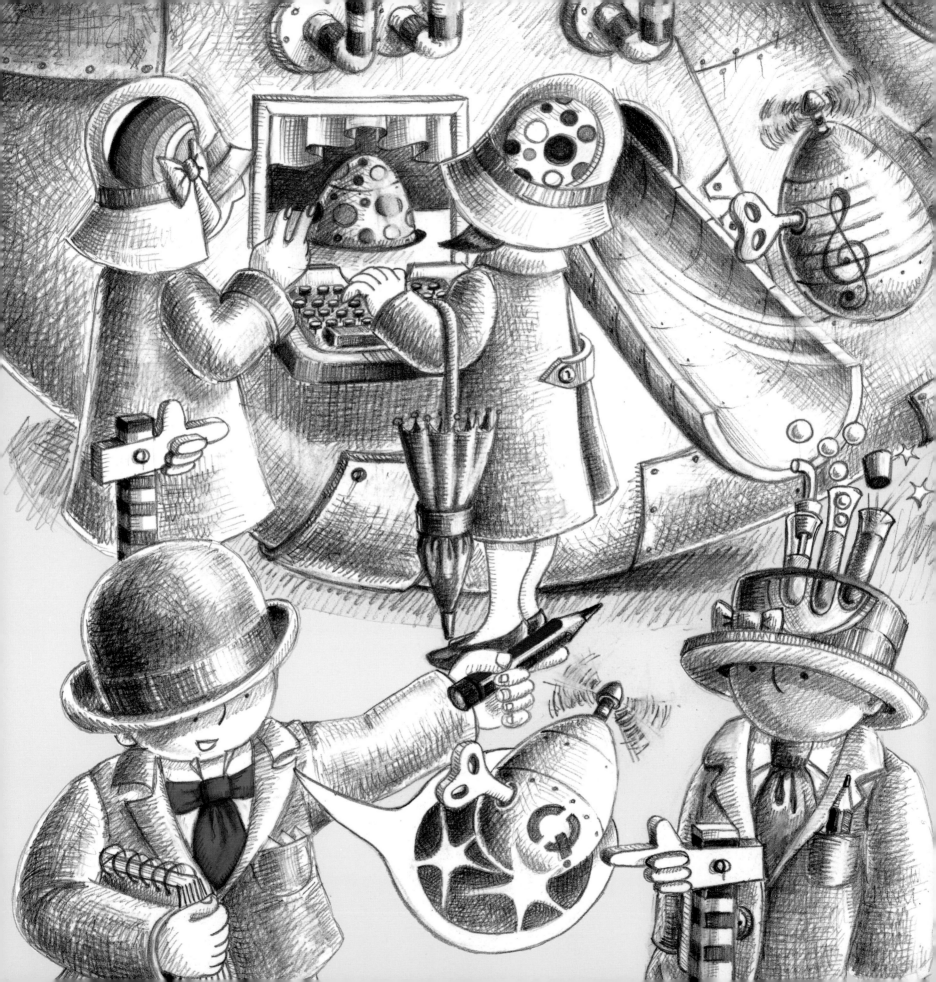

Mr. Qwerty built
the most
EXTRAordinary
thing that anyone
had ever seen.

The world, from that moment on,

was never quite the same.

And Mr. Qwerty
was never alone.